LONGMAN CLASSICS

The Call of the Wild

Jack London

Simplified by Brian Heaton
and D K Swan
Illustrated by Tudor Humphries

Longm

D1124905

Pearson Education Limited,
Edinburgh Gate, Harlow,
Essex CM20 2JE, England
and Associated Companies throughout the world.

This simplified edition © Longman Group UK Limited 1991

First published 1991
This impression Penguin Books 1999

ISBN 0-582-03044-7

Set in 10/13 point Linotron 202 Versailles
Printed in China
GCC/09

Acknowledgements
The cover background is a wallpaper design called
NUAGE, courtesy of Osborne and Little plc.

Stage 4: 1800 word vocabulary
Please look under *New words* at the back of this book
for explanations of words outside this stage.

Contents

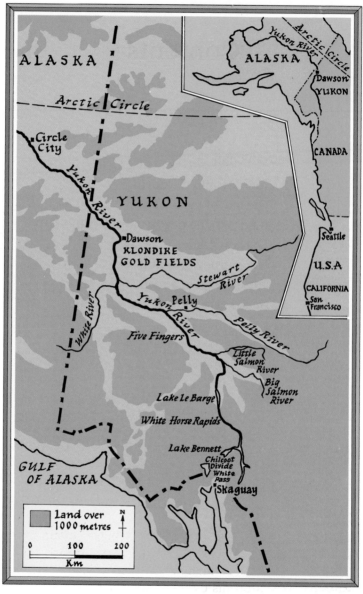

The region of North America where this story takes place

Introduction

Jack London
Jack London was the best-known writer in North America at the beginning of this century. He was born in San Francisco in 1876. He lived for only forty years, but into those years he packed as much experience as most men have in seventy. In the last twenty years he wrote fifty books.

Jack London grew up in the poorest part of Oakland, California. The group of boys he led was often in trouble with the police, and at the age of seventeen he ran away to sea on a ship which hunted seals in the cold seas and ice of the north Pacific Ocean. The terrible experiences of that voyage gave him the background for a novel written ten years later, *The Sea Wolf.*

Back on shore, he became a "hobo", a wanderer without regular work. That experience, including thirty days in prison, was so bad that he made up his mind to educate himself for a better life. He never forgot the other people who were at the very lowest level (the "abyss"), homeless, and treated as worthless. They are presented to us with great sympathy in his *People of the Abyss* (1903) and *The Road* (1907).

London took jobs in food-canning factories and other places of unskilled work to pay his way through high school. It was a time of unbelievably hard work, recorded in a novel based on his own life, *Martin Eden* (1909). His hatred of the way factory owners treated their unskilled workers is expressed in a number of his short stories.

In 1897, Jack London joined the "Gold Rush" to the Klondike in the north-west of Canada. Like most of the 30,000 people who rushed to Dawson and other parts of the Klondike, he got no gold. But the experience gave him material for many of his best short stories. We can read them in collections: *The Son of the Wolf* (1900), *The God of his Fathers* (1901), *Children of the Frost* (1902), *Love of Life* (1907) and *Smoke Bellew* (1912). Two novels about dogs and wolves in the far north, *The Call of the Wild* (1903) and *White Fang* (1906), are considered as classics, dealing with the struggle between the old wild nature and the new civilisation in animals, and – as the reader understands – in human beings.

The Klondike

Gold was discovered at Rabbit Creek in the Klondike in 1896. The great gold rush began in 1897. There was gold in some of the rivers and some was dug out of the ground. By 1910 it was clear that there would be no more lucky "strikes", and only a few deep mines continued to work, although some "prospectors" still search for gold in the wilder parts of Yukon Territory. Some of the people who joined the first gold rush became rich through finding gold – more than one hundred million dollars' worth was taken from the Klondike – and others made fortunes from supplying, transporting or even entertaining the miners.

To get to the Klondike was not easy. In winter, sledges and dog teams followed the "Yukon Trail". In summer, loads could go by the rivers and lakes, but it was necessary to carry goods over mountain passes and between one lake or river and another.

Chapter 1
Journey into the north

Buck did not read the newspapers, so he did not know that trouble was on its way for himself and for every other strong, warm-haired dog. Because men had found a yellow metal called gold, thousands were rushing into the Northland. These men wanted strong, heavy dogs which could work hard and which had long coats to protect them from the snow and ice.

Buck lived at a big house in the sunny Santa Clara Valley in California. The house was called Judge Miller's place. It stood back from the road, half hidden among the trees. The roads to the house passed through wide-spreading lawns and under the branches of tall trees. There were many buildings, green fields and woods.

Buck ruled over all this like a king. The whole place was his. He swam or went hunting with the judge's sons; he stayed at the side of the judge's two daughters on long walks at sunset or in the early morning; on winter nights he lay at the judge's feet in front of the big fire in the library; he carried the judge's grandsons on his back or rolled them in the grass. Among the other dogs of the house he walked proudly, for he was king – king over all living things of Judge Miller's place.

Buck's father, a large St Bernard, had been the judge's close companion. Buck was not so large as his father because his mother, Shep, had been a Scottish shepherd dog; but Buck was able to behave like a true king. Although Buck had great pride, he was not a spoilt house-dog. Hunting and other outdoor delights had kept down the fat and made his body strong.

1

Buck lies at the judge's feet

This was Buck in 1897, when the discovery of gold in the Klondike drew men from all over the world into the frozen north. But Buck did not read the newspapers. Nor did he know that Manuel, one of the gardener's helpers, was a bad man. And Manuel needed money.

One night when the judge and the boys were out, Manuel took Buck for a walk. No one saw them go off through the woods to a small station. At the small station a man talked to Manuel and gave him some money.

Manuel put a piece of thick rope around Buck's neck.

Buck allowed Manuel to put the rope around his neck, for he had learned to trust the men he knew. But when the ends of the rope were placed in the stranger's hands, he growled. To his surprise, the man pulled the rope round his neck, shutting off his breath. In quick anger he sprang at the man, but the man caught hold of him near his throat and, with a quick turn of the hand, threw Buck over on his back. Then he pulled the rope without mercy while Buck struggled angrily, his tongue hanging out of his mouth and his great chest moving up and down without result. He had never in all his life been treated so shamefully, and he had never been so angry. But his strength left him and his eyes closed. He knew nothing when the train arrived and the two men threw him on it.

The next thing he knew was that his tongue was hurting. The noise of the train told him where he was. He had often travelled with the judge and he knew the feeling of riding on a train. He opened his eyes, and anger came into them. The man sprang for his throat, but Buck was too quick for him. His teeth bit the man's hand. They did not stop biting until the rope around his neck was pulled again.

3

The man spoke about that night's ride in a little hut on the San Francisco waterfront.

"I get only fifty for it," he said, "and I wouldn't do it again for a thousand."

There was a bloody handkerchief around his hand.

"I'll give you a hundred and fifty," said the other man. "The dog is worth it."

Buck was unable to think clearly and was suffering great pain. He tried to face the two men, but he was thrown down and the rope was pulled again and again. Then the rope was removed, and he was thrown into a cage.

He lay there for the rest of the long night; he was angry because his pride was wounded. He could not understand what it all meant. What did these strange men want with him? Why were they keeping him a prisoner in this narrow cage? He didn't know why, but he felt that something terrible would happen to him. Several times during the night he sprang to his feet, expecting to see the judge, or the boys. But each time it was the face of a stranger that looked at him by the yellow light of a small candle. And each time the joyful bark in Buck's throat was turned into an angry growl.

In the morning four men entered and picked up the cage. They were evil-looking men; and Buck growled and tried to get at them through the bars. They only laughed and pushed sticks at him. At first he tried to bite the sticks. Then he lay down and allowed them to lift the cage onto a train. Then he, and the cage, began to pass through many hands. Some men in an office took charge of him; he was carried about on another train; he was put on a small ship; he was taken off the ship to a big railway station, and at last he was thrown onto another train.

Buck travelled on this train for two days and nights, and for two days and nights he neither ate nor drank. In his anger he growled at everyone who came to him. When he threw himself against the bars of his cage, they laughed at him. They growled and barked like dogs, made noises like cats, or moved their arms and made noises like birds. He knew that it was all very silly, but it hurt his pride and his anger grew and grew. He did not mind the hunger so much, but he suffered greatly because he had no water.

He was glad about one thing: the rope was off his neck. Now that it was off, he would show them! They would never get another rope around his neck. During those two days and nights he gathered up a great deal of anger. His eyes turned red with blood, and he was changed into a wild devil. He was changed so much that the judge himself would not have known him.

At Seattle, four men carried the cage off the train into a small, high-walled back yard. A fat man came out and signed the book for the driver. Buck threw himself wildly against the bars of the cage. The man smiled cruelly, and brought out an axe and a club.

"You aren't going to take him out now, are you?" the driver asked.

"Certainly," the man replied, driving the axe into the cage to open it.

The four men immediately ran away. They prepared to watch the show from the top of the wall.

Buck rushed at the breaking wood, bit it and struggled with it. He was madly anxious to get out. The man with the axe was calmly trying to get him out.

"Now, you red-eyed devil," he said, when he had made an opening large enough for Buck's body to pass through. At the same time he dropped the axe and moved the club to his right hand.

Buck was truly a red-eyed devil, as he prepared to spring. His hair stood on end, and his red eyes shone with madness. He sprang straight at the man. In mid-air, just as his mouth was about to close on the man, he received a blow that made him shut his mouth in great pain. He fell to the ground on his back. He had never been struck by a club in his life. He did not understand. With a growl of pain he was again on his feet. He sprang at the man, but again the blow came and he was brought to the ground. This time he knew that it was the club; but he was now so angry that he did not care. He charged a dozen times. A dozen times the club struck him down.

After an especially fierce blow, he came slowly to his feet, too tired to rush. He moved without strength, the blood flowing from nose and mouth and ears. His beautiful coat was covered with blood. Then the man advanced and gave him a terrible blow on the nose. All the pain he had suffered was nothing like the great pain he felt now. Buck cried out and again threw himself at the man. But the man, moving the club from right to left, calmly caught him above his throat. At the same time he pulled down and backwards. Buck turned a complete circle in the air; then he fell to the ground on his head and chest.

For the last time he rushed. The man struck the sharp blow which he had kept back on purpose for so long. Buck was helpless; he fell – and knew nothing more.

"He knows how to break in dogs!" cried one of the men on the wall. "He certainly does!"

Buck slowly opened his eyes. He had no strength. He lay where he had fallen. From there he watched the man who had struck him so many times.

6

"He answers to the name of Buck," the man said aloud to himself. He was reading a letter about the cage and Buck. "Well, Buck, my boy," he went on in a friendly voice, "we've had our little trouble. That should be enough. You've learned your place, and I know mine. Be a good dog, and all will go well. Be a bad dog, and I'll beat you without mercy. Do you understand?"

As he spoke he touched without fear the head that he had beaten so hard. Though Buck's hair stood on end at the touch of the hand, he bore it without growling. When the man brought him water, he drank eagerly. Later he ate a big meal of uncooked meat from the man's hand.

He knew that he was beaten, but he was not broken. He saw that he stood no chance against a man with a club. He had learned the lesson, and in all his life he never forgot it. It was his first meeting with the law of the club. Life now had a fiercer look.

As the days went by, other dogs came, in boxes and at the ends of ropes. He watched all of them pass under the power of the man with the club. Again and again, as he looked at each cruel fight, Buck remembered the lesson: a man with a club was a lawgiver and a master to be obeyed. This did not mean that Buck had to like the man, though he did see beaten dogs which showed signs of becoming friendly to the man. Also, he saw one dog, that would neither be friendly nor obey, killed in the struggle.

Now and again men came. They were strangers who talked excitedly to the man with the club. When money passed between them, the strangers took one or more of the dogs away with them. Buck wondered where they went, for they never came back. But he feared the future, and he was glad each time he was not chosen.

Yet Buck's turn came in the end. Perrault was a small man who spoke poor English.

"Eh!" he cried, when he saw Buck. "That's a big, strong dog! How much?"

"Three hundred, and he's a gift at that price," was the quick reply of the man with the club. "And it's government money that you're spending. You can't lose anything, eh, Perrault?"

Perrault smiled. As the price of dogs had risen very high, it was not an unfair amount for so fine an animal. The Canadian government would not lose, and its letters would not travel slower. Perrault knew dogs. When he looked at Buck, he knew that he was one dog in a thousand – "One in ten thousand," he whispered to himself.

Buck saw money pass between the two men. He was not surprised when another dog, called Curly, and he were led away by the small man. That was the last he saw of the man with the club. As Curly and he looked back at Seattle from the ship, it was the last he saw of the warm Southland. Curly and he were taken below by Perrault and given to a man called François. Perrault was French-Canadian, and he had a dark skin; but François, who was also French-Canadian, was twice as dark-skinned. They were a new kind of man to Buck. Although he had no love for them, he learned to respect them. He speedily learned that Perrault and François were fair men, calm and just. They were too wise in the way of dogs to be fooled by dogs.

On the ship, Buck and Curly joined two other dogs. One of them was a big, snow-white fellow from Spitzbergen who had been brought away by a sea-captain. He was called Spitz and was friendly, in an untrustworthy sort of way. He smiled into one's face while he was planning some dishonest trick – as when he stole from Buck's food at the first meal. François struck him before Buck could attack him; and the only thing Buck could do was to take back his bone. Buck decided that François had treated him fairly, and his opinion of him began to rise.

The other dog, called Dave, made no advances, nor received any. Also, he did not attempt to steal from them. He was a dull, unfriendly fellow, and he showed Curly plainly that all he desired was to be left alone. He showed him, too, that there would be trouble if he was not left alone. Dave ate and slept, and took interest in nothing, not even when the ship sailed through rough seas. When Buck and Curly grew excited, half wild with fear, he raised his head as though annoyed, looked at them, and went to sleep again.

Day and night the ship sailed on. One day was very like another, but Buck noticed that the weather was growing colder. At last, one morning, the ship stopped, and everyone on board was excited. Buck felt excited, as did the other dogs, and he knew that a change was near. François put a rope round them, and brought them off the ship. At the first step, Buck's feet went down in something very like mud. It was white and soft. He sprang back with a quick growl. More of this white stuff was falling through the air. He shook himself, but more of it fell on him. He smelt it curiously, then tasted some of it on his tongue. It bit like fire, and the next moment was gone. This puzzled him. He tried it again, with the same result. Those who were watching laughed loudly. It was his first snow.

Chapter 2
The law of the wild

Buck's first day in this new country was like a bad dream. Every hour was filled with sudden surprise. He had suddenly been thrown into the heart of the wild. This was no lazy, sun-kissed life, with nothing to do but waste time. Here there was neither peace, nor rest, nor a moment's safety. It was necessary to be always wide-awake and careful; for these dogs and men were not town dogs and men. They were wild and fierce, all of them, and they knew no law but the law of force.

He had never seen dogs fight as these wolfish creatures fought. His first experience taught him a lesson that he would never forget. It is true that it did not happen to him, or he would be dead. They had camped near the wood store and Curly, in her friendly way, went near a big dog. Suddenly the big dog sprang at Curly. There was the sound of teeth meeting, and the big dog sprang back. Curly's face was cut open from eye to mouth.

It was the wolf manner of fighting, to strike and spring away, but there was more to it than this. Thirty or forty dogs ran to the spot and stood round the two dogs in an eager and silent circle. Buck did not understand that silent eagerness, nor the way their tongues were moving. Curly rushed at the big dog, who struck again and jumped aside. He stopped her next rush with his chest, in a strange way that pushed Curly off her feet. She never got up again. The other dogs had been waiting for this to happen. They jumped on Curly, with excited noises, all barking and growling.

It was so sudden that Buck was surprised. He saw

Spitz laughing; and he saw François, swinging an axe, spring into the crowd of dogs. Three men with clubs were helping him to drive them away. It did not take long. The last of the dogs was driven off two minutes after Curly had fallen down. But she lay there still and lifeless in the blood-covered snow, cut to pieces. The sight of Curly often came back to Buck to trouble him in his sleep. So that was the way. No fair play. Once down, that was the end of you. Well, he would make sure that he never went down. Spitz laughed again, and from that moment Buck felt great hatred towards him.

Soon after the death of Curly, Buck received another surprise. François put a harness on him; the harness was like the ones put on horses at home. And as he had seen horses work, so he was set to work, pulling François on a sledge to the forest and returning with a load of wood. Though this hurt his pride, he was too wise to try to refuse. He began to work eagerly and did his best, though it was all new and strange. François expected everyone to obey him immediately. Dave, who had experience of pulling sledges, bit Buck's back legs whenever he did anything wrong. Spitz was the leader of the dogs and made certain that Buck did his work properly. Buck learned easily and improved quickly. Before they returned to camp he knew enough to stop at the cry, "Ho!", to go forwards at "Mush!", to swing wide round the corners, and to keep clear of the dog behind him when the loaded sledge went downhill.

"These are very good dogs," François told Perrault. "That Buck pulls very hard. I taught him very quickly."

By afternoon, Perrault, who was in a hurry to be off on his journey with his mail, returned with two more dogs.

11

Buck pulls a sledge for the first time

He called them "Billee" and "Joe". Although these two dogs were brothers, they were as different as day and night. Billee's one fault was his good nature, while Joe was the very opposite and was always barking angrily. Buck received them in a friendly manner, but Dave took no notice of them, and Spitz fought first one and then the other. Billee showed no desire to fight, turned to run, and cried when Spitz's sharp teeth bit him. But when Spitz circled, Joe always turned to face him, hair standing on end, ears laid back, lips moving in anger, mouth quickly opening and closing, and with an evil light in his eyes. Joe appeared so terrible that Spitz was forced to stop his attack on him. To save his pride, Spitz turned upon the crying Billee and drove him away.

By evening Perrault had got another dog. He was an old dog, long and thin, with a battle-marked face and a single eye. He was called Sol-leks, which means the Angry One, and other dogs respected him. Like Dave, he asked nothing, gave nothing, expected nothing. When he marched slowly to join them, even Spitz left him alone. There was one strange thing about him that Buck was unlucky enough to discover. He did not like to be approached on his blind side. Not knowing this, Buck went up to Sol-leks in this way. Sol-leks suddenly turned upon Buck and cut his shoulder to the bone for three inches up and down. After this, Buck always kept away from his blind side, and to the end of their friendship he had no more trouble. Sol-leks' only desire, like Dave's, was to be left alone. But, as Buck learnt later, each of them possessed one other, greater desire.

That night Buck had great difficulty in sleeping. The tent looked warm in the middle of the white plain. When he entered it, both Perrault and François shouted angrily at him and threw things at him until he ran away into the cold outside. A cold wind was blowing; it bit into him sharply and made his wounded shoulder very painful. He lay down on the snow and attempted to sleep but the cold soon drove him to his feet. He wandered sadly and hopelessly among the many tents, only to find that one place was as cold as another. Here and there wild dogs rushed upon him, but he growled fiercely (for he was learning fast), and they let him go his way.

At last an idea came to him. He would return and see how the other dogs in the camp were getting along. To his surprise, they had disappeared. Again he wandered about through the great camp, looking for them, and again he returned. Were they in the tent? No, that could not be, or else he would not have been driven out. Then where could they possibly be? Cold and unhappy, he aimlessly circled the tent. Suddenly the snow gave way beneath his front legs and he sank down. Something moved quickly under his feet. He sprang back, angry and growling, frightened of the unseen and unknown. But a friendly little cry removed his fears, and he went back to examine the spot. The smell of warm air reached his nose. There, rolled up under the snow in a warm ball, lay Billee. He barked softly and moved to show his good intentions, and even touched Buck's face with his warm wet tongue.

Buck had learnt another lesson. So that was the way they slept. Buck chose a spot and slowly began to dig a hole for himself. In a moment the heat from his body filled the small space and he was asleep. The day had been long and difficult, and he slept soundly, though he growled and barked and fought with bad dreams.

He did not open his eyes till he was awakened by the noises of the camp. At first he did not know where he was. It had snowed during the night and he was completely covered. The snow walls pressed him on every side, and a great feeling of fear ran through him. It was a wild animal's fear of being caught. His whole body became tight, the hair on his neck and shoulders stood on end, and with a fierce growl he sprang straight up into the blinding day, the snow flying about him in a white cloud. Before he landed on his feet, he saw the white camp spread out in front of him and he knew where he was. He remembered all that had passed from the time he went for a walk with Manuel to the hole he had dug for himself the night before.

A shout from François greeted him. "What did I say?" shouted François to Perrault. "That Buck certainly learns quickly!"

Perrault moved his head in agreement. As a man who carried important messages for the Canadian government, he was anxious to obtain the best dogs, and he was especially pleased with Buck.

Three more dogs were added to the team inside an hour: now there were nine dogs. Before another quarter of an hour had passed they were pulling the sledge towards the Dyea Cañon. Buck was glad to go, and though the work was hard he felt proud doing it. He was surprised that all the dogs were so eager and that he, too, felt eager. Still more surprising was the change in Dave and Sol-leks. They were wide-awake and busy, anxious that the work should go well, and fiercely angry with anything that delayed that work. The work of pulling the sledge seemed to be all that they lived for and the only thing in which they took delight.

Dave was the first dog nearest to the sledge. Pulling in front of Dave was Buck, then came Sol-leks; the rest of the dogs were spread out in front in a single line. Spitz was at the front, leading all the dogs.

Buck had been placed between Dave and Sol-leks on purpose so that he might learn from them. The two dogs were good teachers, never allowing him to make a mistake for long and using their sharp teeth to support their teaching. Dave was fair and very wise. He never bit Buck without cause, and he never failed to bite him when he needed it. François also struck Buck when he made a mistake, so Buck soon learnt. Once, during a short stop, when Buck did something wrong and delayed the start, both Dave and Sol-leks flew at him and bit him. Before the end of the day, Buck had learnt his work so well that his friends stopped biting him. François did not strike him so often, and Perrault even honoured Buck by lifting up his feet and carefully examining them.

It was a hard day's run, up the Cañon, through Sheep Camp, past the Scales and the wood line, across rivers of ice and banks of snow hundreds of feet deep, and over the great Chilcoot Divide, which stands between the salt water and the fresh. They travelled quickly down the chain of lakes, and later that night pulled into the great camp at the head of Lake Bennett. Here thousands of gold-seekers were building boats in preparation for the break-up of the ice in the spring. Buck made his hole in the snow and quickly fell asleep, but early next morning he was pulled out in the cold darkness and put into the harness.

That day they travelled forty miles because the track was good. But the next day, and for many days to follow, there was no track. They had to work harder and they travelled more slowly. Perrault usually travelled in front of the dogs, stamping on the snow to make it easier for them. François, who guided the sledge behind, sometimes changed places with him, but not often. Perrault was in a hurry, and he prided himself on his knowledge of ice. This knowledge was very important, for some of the ice was very thin. Where the water flowed quickly, there was no ice at all.

Day after day, Buck worked as hard as he could, pulling the sledge. They always got up in the dark, and the first grey of daylight found them starting out, leaving fresh miles behind them. And they always set up camp after dark, ate their bit of fish and slept in the snow. Buck was always hungry. The pound and a half of sun-dried fish, which was the amount of food he received each day, seemed far too little. He never had enough, and he suffered from continuous pains of hunger. Yet the other dogs, because they weighed less and were born to the life, received only a pound of the fish and managed to keep in good condition.

He was a slow eater; he found that his friends finished first and then ate his own unfinished food. He could not defend it. While he was fighting two or three, it was disappearing into the mouths of the others. To put an end to this, he ate as fast as they. He was so hungry that he even took what did not belong to him. He watched and learned. When he saw Pike, one of the new dogs, steal a piece of meat behind Perrault's back, he did the same the following day and got away with the whole piece. There was much shouting and noise, but no one thought that Buck was the thief. Another dog, Dub, who was always

17

getting caught, was struck for the deed.

This first act of stealing showed that Buck was fit to take care of himself in this cruel and unfriendly country. It showed that he was able to change himself to fit into changing conditions. If he had been unable to do this, he would have quickly died. It showed that he was losing his respect for the feelings of others and for the things that belonged to them. Whoever kept this respect in the Northland was a fool and would fail in life.

Buck did not reason this out. He was fit, and that was all. Without knowing it, he changed himself to the new way of life. During all his life he had never run from a fight. The man with the club had beaten into him the law of the wild. Before that happened, he could have died in order to defend something that belonged to Judge Miller. Now he was able to forget all finer feelings and so save himself. He did not steal for the joy of it, but because he was hungry. He did not steal openly, but secretly because he respected the law of the wild. The things he did were done because it was easier to do them than not to do them.

His improvement was quick. His body became hard as iron and he did not care about pain. He could eat anything, no matter how bad it was. Once eaten, his stomach got everything from it; and his blood carried it to the farthest parts of his body. His sight and smell became sharp, while his hearing became so good that in his sleep he heard the faintest sound and knew whether it brought peace or danger. He learned to bite the ice with his teeth when it collected at the end of his feet. When he was thirsty and there was a thick covering of ice over the water hole, he broke it by jumping up and striking it with his front legs. The best thing he could do was to smell the wind and tell in what direction it would blow the following day. It did not matter how still the air was when he dug his nest by tree or bank, he was always safe and warm when the wind blew later.

Buck not only learnt by experience, but natural forces and feelings long dead within him became alive again. He remembered back to the youth of his family, to the time when the wild dogs ran about together in packs through the forests and hunted as they ran. It was not difficult for him to learn to fight with his sharp teeth in the manner of a wolf. He felt the old life within him, and the old tricks of the first wolves were his tricks: they came to him naturally, as though they had always been his. And when, on the still cold nights, he pointed his nose at a star and howled long and wolf-like, it was the very first wolves, dead long ago, pointing their noses at a star and howling through the ages and through him. His howls were their howls, that voiced their trouble and sorrow. They voiced the meaning of the stillness, and the cold, and dark.

Thus, the ancient song flowed through him and he came into his own again. He came because men had found a yellow metal in the north, and because Manuel was a gardener's helper who didn't get enough money for the needs of his wife and of himself. Because of that he had come to this wild land, and he had come back to the life of those who lived there and hunted in packs, hundreds of years ago. He had come into his own world again.

Chapter 3
A fight to the death

The spirit of the earliest beasts on earth was strong in Buck; it grew and grew under the fierce conditions of his new life. Yet it was a secret growth. He was too busy changing himself to the new life to feel free from anxiety. Not only did he not pick fights, but he kept away from them whenever possible. He showed a certain carefulness: he did not do anything quickly and without thought. In the great hatred between him and Spitz he suffered everything without complaint and he did nothing to make Spitz angry.

Spitz guessed that Buck was dangerous to him and he showed his teeth in anger whenever he could. He even went out of his way to frighten Buck; he often tried to start the fight which could end only in the death of one or the other. This fight might have come early in the journey if it had not been for an unusual accident.

One evening, they camped on the shore of a great lake. Driving snow, a wind that cut like a white-hot knife, and darkness had forced them to search for a camping place. They could hardly have done worse. At their backs rose a wall of rock. It was necessary for Perrault and François to make their fire and spread their clothes on the ice of the lake itself. They had left their tent behind them in order to travel faster. A few sticks of wood provided them with a fire which soon disappeared through the ice.

Buck made his nest close under the rock. It was so warm and comfortable that he did not want to leave it when François gave out the fish. But when Buck finished eating the fish and returned, he found his nest occupied. An angry growl told him that it was Spitz. Till now Buck had kept away from trouble with his enemy, but this was too much. He sprang upon Spitz with an anger which surprised them both, especially Spitz. Spitz had believed that Buck was an easily frightened dog who was able to protect himself only because of his great weight and size.

François was surprised when they shot out together from the nest. He guessed the cause of the trouble. "A-a-ah!" he cried to Buck. "Give it to him, by God! Give it to him, the dirty thief!"

Spitz was moving in a circle backwards and forwards trying to get a chance to spring in. Buck was no less eager and no less careful, as he also circled back and forth. But just then something happened which no one expected.

There was a shout from Perrault. The crack of a club on a bony body, and a sharp cry of pain were the first signs of what was to follow. The camp was suddenly discovered to be full of hungry dogs. There were eighty or a hundred of them and they had smelled the camp from some Indian village. They had quietly entered the camp while Buck and Spitz were fighting. When the two men sprang among them with heavy clubs they showed their teeth and fought back. The smell of food drove them mad. Perrault found one with its head buried in the food-box. His club landed heavily on the thin body, and the food-box was turned upside down on the ground. In a moment twenty of the hungry beasts were rushing for the bread and meat. They did not pay any attention to the clubs that fell upon them. They cried and howled under the rain of blows, but did not stop struggling till the last piece of bread had been eaten.

While this was happening, the surprised team-dogs had jumped out of their nests and were attacked by the fierce visitors. Buck had never seen such dogs before. It seemed as if their bones would come through their skins. Although they were thin, they were so mad with hunger that they were very frightening. It was impossible to stop them. The team-dogs were driven back against the cliff. Buck was attacked by three of the dogs, and in a moment his head and shoulders were cut and bleeding. The noise was frightful. Billee was crying as usual. Dave and Sol-leks, covered with blood from several wounds, were fighting bravely side by side. Joe was attacking the dogs like a devil. Buck got one of the dogs by the throat, and was covered with blood when his teeth sank through the skin. The warm taste of it in his mouth made him become even fiercer. He threw himself upon another, and at the same time felt teeth sink into his own throat. It was Spitz, attacking him from the side.

After Perrault and François had cleaned out their part of the camp, they hurried to save their dogs. The hungry attackers ran away from them, and Buck shook himself free. But it was only for a moment. The two men were forced to run back to save the food, and the hungry dogs returned to the attack on the team. Billee sprang through the circle of dogs and ran away over the ice. Pike and Dub followed him, with the rest of the camp-dogs behind. As Buck got ready to spring after them, he saw Spitz out of the corner of his eye. Spitz was rushing upon him with the intention of throwing him off his feet. Once off his feet and under that crowd of hungry dogs, there was no hope for Buck. But he gathered up his strength and stood firm. Then he ran after the other team-dogs out on the lake.

Later, the nine team-dogs gathered together and looked for a safe place to rest in the forest. Though they were not pursued, they were in a bad state. Each of them was wounded in four or five places, while some were wounded very badly indeed. Dub was badly hurt in a back leg; Dolly, the last dog added to the team at Dyea, had a badly torn throat; Joe had lost an eye; and Billee, whose ear was bitten into small pieces, cried all night. When it was daylight, they walked slowly back to camp. Their attackers had gone, and the two men were angry. Half of their food supply was lost. The attackers had even bitten through the sledge ropes and the covers. In fact, nothing had escaped them; they had eaten everything that it was at all possible to eat.

"Ah, my friends," François said softly when he looked over his wounded dogs, "perhaps so many bites will make you mad dogs. Perhaps you are all mad dogs. What do you think, Perrault?"

Perrault shook his head doubtfully. With four hundred miles still between him and Dawson, he could not bear the thought that madness might break out among his dogs.

After two hours' hard work, the wounded team was on its way again. They struggled painfully over the hardest part of the journey.

The Thirty Mile River was wide open: its wild water was not frozen. There was ice only in the quiet places near the sides. Six days of tiring work were needed to cover those thirty terrible miles. And terrible they were, for every foot of them was gained only at the danger of loss of life to dog and man. Perrault, who was trying to find the way, broke through the ice bridges many times.

He was saved only by the long stick he carried. He held it in such a way that it fell each time across the hole made by his body. But it was very cold indeed. Each time Perrault fell through the ice he had to build a fire and dry his clothes in order to stay alive.

Nothing frightened Perrault. It was because nothing frightened him that he had been chosen to carry the government mail. He passed through all kinds of danger, struggling on from dim daylight to dark. He walked round the shores of the great river on ice that started to crack underfoot. It was so thin that they dared not stop. Once, the sledge broke through the ice, with Dave and Buck. They were half-frozen and almost drowned by the time they were pulled out. A fire was necessary to save them. They were thickly coated with ice. The two men made them run so close around the fire that they were nearly burnt.

At another time Spitz went through, pulling the whole team after him up to Buck. Buck pulled backwards with all his strength, his front feet on the edge and the ice cracking all around. But behind him was Dave, also pulling backwards, and behind the sledge was François pulling as hard as he could.

Again, the ice broke away before and behind, and there was no escape except up the cliff. Perrault surprised everyone by climbing the cliff. Every sledge rope and piece of harness was tied into a long rope. The dogs were pulled up, one by one, to the top of the cliff. François came up last, after the sledge and load. Then came the search for a place to descend. They got down at last with the aid of the rope, and night found them back on the river only a quarter of a mile further on.

By the time they reached good ice, Buck was tired out.

The rest of the dogs were in the same condition. But Perrault pushed them hard to make up lost time. The first day they covered thirty-five miles to the Big Salmon River; the next day thirty-five more to the Little Salmon; the third day forty miles, which brought them well up towards a place called Five Fingers.

Buck's feet were not so firm and hard as the feet of many other dogs. All day long he walked about in great pain. Once camp was made, he lay down like a dead dog. Even though he was hungry, he would not move to receive his amount of fish, which François had to bring to him. Also, François rubbed Buck's feet for half an hour each night after supper, and used the tops of his own warm shoes to make four shoes for Buck. This was a great comfort, and Buck caused even Perrault to smile one morning – when François forgot the shoes. Buck lay on his back, with his four feet waving in the air, and refused to move without them. Later his feet grew hard, and the worn-out shoes were thrown away.

At the Pelly River one morning, as they were harnessing up, Dolly suddenly went mad. No one had ever taken much notice of her before. She showed her madness by a long, wolf howl that filled every dog with fear. Then she sprang straight for Buck. He had never seen a dog go mad, nor did he have any reason to fear madness. But he knew that here was something terrible, and fled from it.

He raced away, with Dolly one jump behind. She could not gain on him, so great was his terror. Nor could he leave her, so great was her madness. He ran through the wooded part of the island, came down to the lower end, crossed over some rough ice to another island, reached a third island, turned back to the main river, and started to cross it. And all the time he could hear her growling with rage just one jump behind.

François called to him a quarter of a mile away and he ran back, still one jump in front. He put all his faith in François, hoping that he would save him. François held the axe ready in his hand. As Buck shot past him, the axe fell down upon mad Dolly's head.

Buck lay down against the sledge, tired out, crying for breath, helpless. This was Spitz's chance. He sprang upon Buck. Twice his teeth bit into Buck and cut down to the bone. Then François's whip descended, and Buck watched Spitz receive the worst whipping he had ever seen.

"That Spitz is a devil," said Perrault. "Some day he will kill Buck."

"Buck is like two devils," said François. "I know this for sure. I watch that Buck all the time and I know! Listen! Some day Buck will get really angry and eat up Spitz: eat him all up. Sure! I know."

From then on it was war between Spitz and Buck. Although Spitz was the lead-dog and master of the team, he felt danger from this strange Southland dog. And Buck was certainly strange to him. Spitz had known many Southland dogs but not one had shown itself to be worth his respect in camp and on the journeys. They were all too soft; they died from the hard work, the cold, and hunger. Buck was different. He alone suffered and never complained; he alone succeeded and proved himself as strong and wild as any other dog. Buck was dangerous because the man with the club had knocked all blind courage out of him. Buck was especially good at deceiving people and he was able to wait calmly to get what he wanted.

The fight for leadership was sure to come. Buck wanted it. He wanted it because it was his nature. He was caught by that nameless pride of the north – that pride which keeps dogs struggling on until they die. It is the pride which leads them to die joyfully in the harness and breaks their hearts if they are cut out of the harness. It was the pride that laid hold of them as soon as they left the camp, changing them from unfriendly beasts into hard-working and eager creatures. It was the pride that kept them going all day and dropped them at night when camp was set up. This was the pride that made Spitz bite the sledge-dogs who made mistakes and were lazy. Also, it was this pride that made Spitz fear Buck as a possible lead-dog. And this was Buck's pride, too.

He stood up to Spitz and protected the dogs who had made mistakes. And he did it calmly and firmly. One night there was a heavy snowfall, and in the morning Pike, the lazy dog who was always pretending to be ill, did not appear. Pike was safely hidden in his nest under a foot of snow. François called him and searched for him without success. Spitz was wild with anger. He ran through the camp, smelling and digging in every possible place. He growled so fiercely that Pike heard and shook in his hiding-place.

When Spitz at last found Pike and flew at him, Buck flew, with equal anger, between the two dogs. It was so unexpected that Spitz was thrown backwards and off his feet. Pike, who had been shaking with fear, gained courage at this event and sprang upon Spitz. Buck also sprang upon Spitz. But François brought his whip down upon Buck with all his strength. This failed to drive Buck away, and the thick end of the whip was used. Buck was knocked backwards and he was whipped again and again.

In the days that followed, Buck still continued to defend the other dogs against Spitz. But he did it in secret, when François was not there. The other dogs began to lose their respect for Spitz and even disobey him. Dave and Sol-leks remained faithful, but the rest of the team went from bad to worse. Things no longer went right. There was a lot of noisy quarrelling. Trouble was always present, and at the bottom of it was Buck. He kept François busy, for François now lived in fear of the life-and-death struggle between the two dogs; he knew this struggle must come sooner or later. On more than one night the sounds of quarrelling among the other dogs caused him to leave his bed, fearing that Buck and Spitz were fighting.

But there was no suitable chance, and they reached Dawson one cold afternoon with the fight still to come. There were many men and dogs in Dawson, and Buck found them all at work. It seemed the natural order of things that dogs should work. All day they swung up and down the main street in long teams. Their bells still sounded in the night as they went by. They pulled loads of wood, carried things up to the mines, and did all kinds of work that horses did in the Santa Clara Valley. Here and there Buck met Southland dogs, but most of the dogs were the wild wōlf kind. Every night, regularly, at nine, at twelve, at three, they all howled. It was a strange song of the night, and it was Buck's delight to join in it.

With the northern lights shining coldly above, or the stars dancing, and the land frozen under its covering of snow, this song of the dogs put into words the pain of living. It was an old song, old as life itself – one of the first songs in a younger world when songs were sad. The

The dogs howl at night

sorrow of thousands of years was in this song, which moved Buck so strangely. When he howled, it was with the pain of living that was the pain of his wild fathers. When he cried, it was with the fear and mystery of the cold and dark, the fear and mystery that his wild fathers had felt long ago. When he felt that mystery and howled, he had gone back through time to the beginnings of life.

Seven days after they arrived at Dawson, they dropped down a steep bank to the Yukon Trail, and set out for Dyea and Salt Water. Perrault was carrying mail which was even more important than the mail he had brought to Dawson. Also, the travel-pride caught hold of him, and he intended to make the fastest journey of the year. Several things favoured him in this. The week's rest had made the dogs fresh again and put them in good condition. Their journey was easier. In two or three places the police had arranged stores of food for dog and man, and Perrault was travelling without many things to carry.

They reached the place called Sixty Mile, which is a fifty-mile run, on the first day. The second day saw them coming up the Yukon River, well on their way to Pelly. But such splendid running was gained only with great difficulty on the part of François. Buck had destroyed the spirit of the team. The team was no longer like one dog pulling the sledge. Buck led the dogs into all kinds of wrongdoing. Spitz was no longer greatly feared. Pike stole half a fish from him one night, and ate it under the protection of Buck. Another night Dub and Joe fought Spitz. Even Billee, the good-natured, was less good-natured. Buck never came near Spitz without growling angrily. In fact, he began to use his strength to frighten Spitz and he walked proudly up and down before Spitz's very nose.

The breaking down of respect and order made the dogs quarrel more than ever among themselves. At times the camp was full of their howls. Dave and Sol-leks alone remained the same, though they were easily made angry by the quarrelling. François shouted and stamped about in the snow in useless anger and tore his hair. He whipped the dogs, but it was of little use. As soon as his back was turned, they were quarrelling again. He supported Spitz with his whip, while Buck helped the rest of the team. François knew that Buck was the cause of all the trouble, and Buck knew that he knew. But Buck was too clever to be caught. He worked hard, for the work had become a delight to him. But it was a greater delight to start a fight among his friends.

One night after supper, Dub found a rabbit. The rabbit was too quick for him and escaped. In a second the whole team was pursuing the rabbit. There was a camp of the Northwest Police a hundred yards away, with fifty dogs: they all joined the pursuit. The rabbit ran down the river and then turned off into a small bay. It ran lightly on top of the snow, while the dogs forced their way through the snow by their great strength. Buck led the pack – sixty dogs – but he could not gain. He raced on, his splendid body springing forward in the white light of the moon. And jump by jump, the rabbit ran in front of him.

The old spirit which at certain times drives men out from the big cities to the forests and plains to hunt and shoot things, the love for blood, the joy to kill – all this was Buck's. He was running at the head of the pack, hunting the wild thing down, the living meat. He would kill it with his own teeth and wash his mouth in warm blood.

There is a great joy which marks the highest point of life. This joy comes when one is most alive. Yet the fact of being alive is completely forgotten. This joy comes to the artist who forgets himself in what he is doing. It comes to the soldier who refuses to run away from a losing battle. And it came to Buck, leading the pack, howling like a wolf, running after the food that was alive and that fled before him through the moonlight. Buck was mastered by the sheer joy of life, expressing itself in movement, flying under the stars and over the dead ground beneath.

But Spitz, cold and always calm, left the pack and cut across a narrow neck of land. Buck did not know of this, and as he ran after the rabbit, he saw another and larger shape spring from the bank of the river in front of the rabbit. It was Spitz. The rabbit could not turn. As Spitz's white teeth broke the rabbit's back in mid-air, it cried out as loudly as a dying man. At the sound of this, the pack behind Buck raised a cry of delight.

Buck did not cry out. He did not stop himself, but drove in upon Spitz, shoulder to shoulder, so hard that he missed the throat. They rolled over and over in the snow. Spitz gained his feet almost as though he had not been thrown over. He bit Buck on the shoulder and jumped clear. Twice his teeth came together, like a steel trap, as he backed away.

In a second Buck knew it. The time had come. It was a fight to the death. As they circled about, growling angrily, ears laid back, carefully watching each other, Buck felt that he had known this scene before. He seemed to remember it all – the white woods, and earth, and moonlight, and the joy of battle. A ghostly calm hung over the whiteness and silence. There was not the faintest

Buck fights Spitz

movement of air. Nothing moved, not even a leaf. The breath of the dogs rose slowly in the cold air. They had soon eaten the rabbit, these dogs that were really wolves. Now they were drawn up in a circle. They, too, were silent, their eyes shining and their breath moving slowly up in the air. To Buck it was nothing new or strange – it was a scene of old time. It was as though it had always been, the usual way of things.

Spitz had fought many times before. From Spitz-bergen through the Arctic, and across Canada, he had gained command over all kinds of dogs. His anger was fierce, but it was never blind. Even when he was mastered by his strong feelings to tear and destroy, he never forgot that his enemy felt the same way. He never rushed till he was prepared to receive a rush; he never attacked till he had first defended that attack.

Buck tried without success to bite the neck of the big white dog. Whenever his sharp teeth struck for the softer places, they were met by the teeth of Spitz. Tooth hit tooth, and lips were cut and covered with blood, but Buck could not succeed in his attacks. Then he warmed up and rushed for Spitz many times. Time and time again he tried for the snow-white throat. Each time and every time Spitz cut him and got away. Then Buck began to rush, as though for the throat. Suddenly drawing back his head and turning in from the side, he drove his shoulder at the shoulder of Spitz to throw him over. But instead, Buck's shoulder was cut each time as Spitz sprang lightly away.

Spitz was not touched, while Buck was covered with blood and breathing hard and fast. Hope was leaving Buck. All the time the silent, wolfish circle waited to finish off the dog which went down. As Buck grew short of breath, Spitz started rushing, and he made it difficult for Buck to stand. Once Buck went over, and the whole circle of sixty dogs started up. But he jumped to his feet, almost in mid-air, and the circle sat down again and waited.

But Buck possessed something that helped towards greatness – imagination. He fought naturally without thinking, but he could fight with his head as well. He rushed as though attempting the old shoulder trick, but at the last moment he went low to the snow and in. His teeth closed on Spitz's left front leg. There was the sound of breaking bone, and Spitz faced him on three legs. Three times Buck tried to knock him over; then he repeated the trick and broke the right front leg. Though full of pain and helpless, Spitz struggled madly to keep up. He saw the silent circle, with shining eyes and tongues hanging out. He saw them closing in on him as he had seen other circles close in on beaten fighters in the past. But this time he was the one who was beaten.

There was no hope for him. Buck could not turn aside from the task. Mercy was a thing for gentler lands. He prepared for the last rush. The circle had moved slowly in till he could feel the breath of the dogs on his body. He could see them, beyond Spitz and to either side, ready for the spring, their eyes fixed upon him. Something seemed to stop all movement. Every animal stood still as though turned to stone. Only Spitz moved as he tried to walk back and forth, growling fiercely as though to frighten off death. Then Buck sprang in and out. The dark circle moved forwards as Spitz disappeared from view.

Buck stood and looked on, the successful leader who had made his kill and found it good.

Chapter 4
The new leader

"Eh? What did I say? I spoke the truth when I said that Buck was like two devils."

This was what François said next morning when he discovered Spitz missing and Buck covered with wounds. He drew him to the fire and by its light pointed them out.

"That Spitz fought very fiercely," said Perrault, as he examined the cuts on Buck's body.

"And that Buck fought even more fiercely," François answered. "And now we can travel faster. No more Spitz, no more trouble!"

While Perrault loaded the sledge, François began to harness the dogs. Buck walked up to Spitz's old place as leader. But François did not notice him and brought Sol-leks to the place at the front of the team. In his judgement, Sol-leks was the best lead-dog left. Buck sprang upon Sol-leks in great anger, driving him back and standing in his place.

"Eh? eh?" François cried. "Look at that Buck. He has killed Spitz, and he wants to take his job."

"Go away, Buck!" he cried, but Buck refused to move.

François took Buck by the neck. Though Buck growled angrily, François pulled him to one side and put Sol-leks back. Sol-leks did not like it, and showed plainly that he was afraid of Buck. François meant to keep Sol-leks at the front, but when he turned his back, Buck again took the place of Sol-leks, who was very willing to go.

François was angry. "Now, by God, I'll fix you!" he cried, coming back with a heavy club in his hand.

Buck remembered the fat man in the yard, and walked

slowly back. He did not attempt to attack when Sol-leks was once more brought forward. But he walked round in a circle just beyond the range of the club, growling with fierce anger. While he circled he watched the club so as to move quickly away if François threw it. He had become wise in the way of clubs.

François went on with his work. He called to Buck when he was ready to put him in his old place in front of Dave. Buck drew back two or three steps. François followed him and he again drew back. After some time of this, François threw down the club, thinking that Buck feared being hit. But Buck refused to obey. He wanted, not to escape being hit, but to be the leader of the team. This was his right. He had won it and he would not be satisfied with less.

Perrault helped François. The two men ran after Buck for nearly an hour. They threw clubs at him. He moved out of the way. They shouted at him and cursed him and his fathers and mothers before him. But Buck answered their shouts with angry growls and kept out of their reach. He did not try to run away, but went around and around the camp. He showed plainly that he would come in and be good when his desire to lead was answered.

François sat down and scratched his head. Perrault looked at his watch and spoke angrily. Time was flying, and they should have started off an hour ago. François scratched his head again. He shook it and smiled at Perrault. Perrault moved his shoulders in a sign that they were beaten. Then François went up to where Sol-leks stood and called to Buck. Buck laughed, as dogs laugh, yet stayed a few feet away from them. François put Sol-leks back in his old place. The team stood harnessed to the sledge in a line, ready to go. There was no place for

37

Buck except at the front. Once more François called, and once more Buck laughed and kept away.

"Throw down the club," Perrault commanded.

François threw down the club and Buck walked in. He swung around into place at the head of the team. His harness was put on; the sledge started off, and they hurried out on to the frozen river.

Though François had valued Buck highly in the past, he soon found that Buck was even better than he had thought. At once Buck took up the duties of leading. When judgement was needed and quick thinking and quick acting, he showed himself even better than Spitz.

But Buck was best at giving the law and making the other dogs live up to it. Dave and Sol-leks did not mind the change of leader. It was none of their business. Their business was to work hard pulling the sledge. So long as Buck did not touch them, they did not care what happened. Billee, the good-natured, could lead for all they cared, so long as he kept order. The rest of the team, however, had got out of order during the last days of Spitz; they were very surprised now that Buck began to make them work hard.

Pike, who pulled behind Buck and who never really did any work, was quickly shaken for being lazy. Before the end of the first day he was pulling more than ever before in his life. The first night in camp, Joe, the unfriendly one, was beaten until he began to cry out for mercy: Buck simply lay on top of him.

The team began to improve immediately. Once more the dogs ran as one dog in front of the sledge. Soon two new dogs, Teek and Koona, were added. The speed with which Buck trained them was a big surprise to François.

"I've never seen such a dog as that Buck!" he cried. "No, never! He's worth one thousand dollars, by God! Eh? What do you say, Perrault?"

And Perrault agreed. He was beating the record time for the journey, and he was gaining day by day.

The snow-covered ground was in excellent condition: it was very hard and there was no new-fallen snow. It was not too cold. The men rode and ran by turn, and the dogs were kept going all the time.

There was a lot of ice over the Thirty Mile River; they covered in one day the same distance that had before taken them ten days. In one run they travelled sixty miles from the foot of Lake Le Barge to the White Horse Rapids. They flew quickly over seventy miles of lakes. On the last night of the second week they passed over White Pass and dropped down to Skaguay and to the sea.

It was a record run. Each day for fourteen days they had travelled about forty miles. For three days Perrault and François walked up and down the main street of Skaguay, throwing their chests out with pride. Everyone asked them to drink with them, and the team received a lot of attention from a respectful crowd of dog-drivers in the town. Then three or four bad men attempted to steal money from the town. They were killed, and public interest turned from the dogs to these men. Next came orders from the government. François called Buck to him, threw his arms around him, and wept over him. And this was the last of François and Perrault. Like other men, they passed out of Buck's life.

In company with twelve other dogs Buck started back on the long journey to Dawson. It was not easy running now, nor record time, but hard work each day, with a heavy load behind. This was the mail train, carrying news from the world to the men who sought gold under the shadow of the North Pole.

Buck did not like it, but he bore up well to the work. He took pride in it like Dave and Sol-leks, and he made sure that the other dogs did their fair share of work whether they took pride in it or not. It was not at all an interesting life: one day was very like another. At a certain time each morning the cooks got up, fires were built, and breakfast was eaten. Then, while some got everything ready to take on the journey, others harnessed the dogs. They were off an hour or so before dawn. At night, camp was made. Some set up the little tents, others cut firewood and branches for the beds, and others carried water or ice for the cooks. Also the dogs were fed. This was the best part of the day to the dogs, though it was also good to stand around for an hour or so with the other dogs after the fish was eaten. There were fierce fighters among them. Buck gained respect after three battles with the fiercest. In future, when he became angry and showed his teeth, they got out of his way.

Best of all, Buck loved to lie near the fire, looking dreamily at the burning wood. Sometimes he thought of Judge Miller's big house in the sun-kissed Santa Clara Valley. But more often he remembered the man with the club, the death of Curly, the great fight with Spitz, and the good things he had eaten or would like to eat. He never felt eager to return home. The Sunland was very dim and far away, and such memories had no power over him. The memories of his ancient family had far more power: he seemed to know about things he had never seen before. Old feelings became alive again.

It was a hard journey: the heavy work of pulling the mail wore the dogs down. They were very tired and weak and thin when they reached Dawson. They should have had ten days' or a week's rest at least. But after two days in Dawson, they went back along the Yukon, loaded with letters for the outside world. The dogs were tired and the drivers were always complaining. To make matters worse, it snowed every day. This meant that the snow-covered ground was soft, and it was harder for the dogs to pull the sledge. Yet the drivers were always fair and did their best for the animals.

Each night the dogs were attended to first. They ate before the drivers ate. No man went to sleep before he had examined the feet of the dogs he drove. But their strength went down. Since the beginning of the winter they had travelled eighteen hundred miles, pulling sledges all the time. Eighteen hundred miles make even the strongest dog grow weak. Buck bore up to it all. He kept the other dogs up to their work though he, too, was very tired. Billee cried often in his sleep each night. Joe was more unfriendly than ever, and Sol-leks never allowed anyone to come near him.

But it was Dave who suffered most of all. Something had gone wrong with him. He became unfriendly and was easily made angry. When camp was set up, he at once made his nest in the place where his driver fed him. Once out of the harness and down, he did not get on his feet again until they were ready to set off the next morning. Sometimes, when the sledge suddenly stuck in the ice, Dave would cry out with pain. The driver examined him, but could find nothing. All the drivers became interested in what was happening to him. They talked about it during meals and before going to bed. One night they talked for a long time. Dave was brought from his nest to the fire. He was pressed till he cried out many times. Something was wrong inside, but they could find no broken bones and could not understand his illness.

Soon Dave was so weak that he was falling again and again as he pulled the sledge. He was taken out of the team so that he could rest and run free behind the sledge. Though he was sick, Dave did not like being taken out of the team. He cried sadly when he saw Sol-leks being put in his place, for Dave had great pride in his work and, though he was almost dying, he could not bear to see another dog doing his work.

When the sledge started, Dave struggled in the soft snow at the side of the sledge and attacked Sol-leks with his teeth. He rushed against him and tried to throw him off into the soft snow on the other side. All the time he was crying with grief and pain. The men tried to drive him away with the whip. Dave took no notice of it and the men couldn't bear to strike harder. He refused to run quietly behind the sledge, where the snow was hard and it was easy to run. Instead, he continued to struggle at the side in the soft snow. At last he fell and lay where he fell, crying unhappily as the long train of sledges passed by.

With the last of his strength he ran along behind till the train of sledges made another stop. Then he struggled past the sledges to his own, and stood at the side of Sol-leks. His driver waited a moment to get a light for his pipe from the man behind. Then he returned and started his dogs. They set off quickly and easily; then they turned their heads and stopped in surprise. The driver was surprised, too; the sledge had not moved. He called his friends to see the sight. Dave had bitten through the

Dave struggles in the soft snow

harness and was standing in front of the sledge in his proper place.

He begged with his eyes to remain there. The driver was puzzled. His friends said, "A dog can break its heart if it is not allowed to do its work." Since Dave was dying, the drivers thought that it would be a mercy for him to die in his proper place in front of the sledge. So he was put in the harness again. Though more than once he cried out with pain, he pulled proudly as in the past. Several times he fell down; once the sledge ran onto him and hurt one of his legs.

But he succeeded in pulling the sledge till they reached camp. His driver made a place for him by the fire, but the next morning he was too weak to travel. He tried to walk to his driver but fell. Then he moved slowly on his stomach towards the sledge. He first moved his front legs forward and drew up his body a few inches. His strength left him: he lay on the snow. That was the last the other dogs saw of him. But they could hear him howling with grief till they passed out of sight behind some trees.

Here the sledges stopped. One of the men slowly walked back to the camp that they had left. The other men ceased talking. A shot rang out. The sledges moved once more. But Buck knew, and every dog knew, what had happened behind the trees.

Chapter 5
The journey of death

The Salt Water Mail, with Buck and his companions pulling it, arrived at Skaguay thirty days after leaving Dawson. The dogs were in a poor state; they were worn out. Buck's weight of one hundred and forty pounds had gone down to one hundred and fifteen. The rest of his companions, though lighter dogs, had lost more weight. Pike, who had often pretended to have a hurt leg, now really did have a hurt leg. Sol-leks could no longer walk properly and Dub was suffering from a painful shoulder. They all had painful feet.

"Run on, poor feet," the driver shouted kindly when they ran down the main street of Skaguay. "This is the last. Then we'll get a long rest. A very long rest."

The drivers expected a long rest. They had covered twelve hundred miles with two days' rest: they deserved a rest. But the men had orders. New dogs were to take the places of those who were tired and useless. The useless ones were to be sold.

Three days passed, by which time Buck and his companions found how really tired and weak they were. Then, on the morning of the fourth day, two men came along and bought them at a very low price. The men addressed each other as "Hal" and "Charles". Charles was a man of between forty and fifty, with watery eyes and a weak lip. Hal was a young man of nineteen or twenty. He had a big gun and a hunting knife on his belt.

They overloaded their sledge and then tried to start. The dogs sprang forwards, pulled hard for a few moments, then stopped. They were unable to move the sledge.

"The lazy beasts, I'll show them," Hal cried, preparing to strike them with the whip.

"They're weak as water," said a man from the next tent. "They're worn out. They need a rest."

"They'll not get a rest," said Hal. "Mush!" he shouted. "Mush on there!"

His whip fell on the dogs.

One of the men who was looking on now spoke up.

"I don't care at all what happens to you, but I do care about the dogs. You can help them a great deal by breaking the ice around that sledge. It's frozen fast in the ice. Throw your weight against it and break it out."

Hal followed the advice and pushed his weight against the sledge. The heavy sledge slowly moved forwards. Buck and his companions struggled under the rain of blows from Hal's whip.

The dogs struggled on, whipped and beaten, day after day. They had no life in them when they entered John Thornton's camp at the mouth of the White River. When they stopped, the dogs dropped down as though they had all been struck dead. John Thornton was finishing an axe that he had made. He listened, gave simple replies and a few words of advice when it was asked. He knew what kind of people they were and he was certain that his advice would not be followed.

"They told us up above that the ice was disappearing and that the best thing for us to do was to stop for a time," Hal said after Thornton had advised them to take no more chances on the ice. Hal continued, "They told us we couldn't reach White River, and here we are."

"And they told you true," John Thornton answered. "The ice may break at any moment. Only fools would have attempted to do it. I tell you straight: I wouldn't go on that ice for all the gold in Alaska."

"That's because you're not a fool, I suppose," said Hal. "All the same, we'll go on to Dawson." He held out his whip. "Get up there, Buck! Hi! Get up there! Mush on!"

But the team did not get up at the command. It had long since become necessary to whip the team in order to make them start. John Thornton bit his lips. Sol-leks was the first to struggle to his feet. Teek followed. Joe came next, barking with pain. Pike tried hard to stand. Twice he fell over when he was half up. On the third attempt he succeeded in rising. Buck made no effort. He lay quietly where he had fallen. The whip bit into him again and again, but he neither cried out nor struggled.

This was the first time Buck had failed. This in itself was enough to make Hal very angry. He changed the whip for a club. Buck refused to move under the rain of heavier blows which now fell upon him. He had made up his mind not to get up. He had a feeling that some terrible accident was about to happen out there on the ice where his master was trying to drive him. As the blows continued to fall upon him, the faint trace of life within nearly disappeared. He knew that he was being beaten, but it was as though from a great distance. He no longer felt anything, though very faintly he could hear the sound of the club upon his body. But it was no longer his body; it seemed so far away.

And then, suddenly, making a cry that was like the cry of an animal, Thornton sprang upon the man who was hitting Buck with the club. Hal was thrown backwards, as though struck by a falling tree. Charles looked on but did not get up to help Hal.

John Thornton stood over Buck, too angry to speak.

"If you strike that dog again, I'll kill you," he said.

"It's my dog," Hal replied, drying the blood from his mouth as he came back. "Get out of my way, or I'll kill *you*. I'm going to Dawson."

Thornton stood between him and Buck and showed that he had no intention of getting out of the way. Hal drew his long hunting knife. Thornton hit the back of Hal's hand with a stick, knocking the knife to the ground. He hit his hands again as Hal tried to pick it up. Then he picked it up himself and quickly cut Buck's harness.

Hal had neither the strength nor the spirit to fight any more. Buck was too near dead to be of further use in pulling the sledge. A few minutes later the rest of the team started out from the bank and went down the river. Buck heard them go and raised his head to see. Pike was leading; then came Joe, Teek and Sol-leks. Hal guided, and Charles walked along in the rear.

As Buck watched them, Thornton knelt beside him and felt him for broken bones. He could find nothing wrong except for many wounds and a state of great hunger. By the time he had finished examining Buck, the sledge was a quarter of a mile away. The dog and the man watched it moving slowly along over the ice. Suddenly, they saw its back end drop down into a small hole. They saw Charles turn and make one step to run back. Then a large piece of ice broke and dogs and men disappeared. A wide and deep hole was all that was to be seen.

John Thornton and Buck looked at each other.

"You poor devil," said John Thornton, and Buck ran his tongue along his new master's hand.

Chapter 6
For the love of a man

When John Thornton's feet froze during the winter just before he met Buck, his friends had made him comfortable and left him to get well. They themselves went on up the river. John Thornton was still walking with slight difficulty at the time he saved Buck, but the continued warm weather made his feet completely well again. And Buck lay by the river bank through the long spring days and slowly won back his strength.

A rest feels very good after one has travelled three thousand miles, and Buck even grew a little lazy as his wounds healed and his body grew strong again. Indeed, they were all lazy – Buck, John Thornton, and Skeet and Nig, as they waited for the canoe to come to carry them down to Dawson. Skeet was a small dog who soon made friends with Buck. She had acted almost like a doctor to Buck; and, as a mother cat washes her young, so she washed Buck's wounds. Each morning after he had finished his breakfast, she attended to Buck. Nig, equally friendly, was a large black dog, with eyes that laughed.

John Thornton had saved Buck's life; but, as well as that, he was the perfect master. Other men looked after their dogs from a feeling of duty and in the interests of business. John Thornton looked after his dogs as if they were his own children, because he could not help it. He had a way of taking Buck's head roughly between his hands, and resting his own head on Buck's. He would shake Buck, all the time calling him bad names which to Buck were love names. Buck knew no greater joy than this.

Buck with Thornton

But though Buck loved John Thornton deeply, the call of the wild, which the Northland had awakened in him, remained alive. Thornton alone held him. Other men might praise him or touch him, but he was cold under it all, and often he got up and walked away. When Thornton's friends, Hans and Pete, arrived on the long-expected canoe, Buck refused to notice them till he learnt that they were close to Thornton. After that, he did not mind them, but at the same time he showed no real feeling for them. They were the same kind of men as Thornton, living close to the earth, thinking simply and seeing clearly. Before the canoe reached Dawson, they understood Buck and his ways.

Buck's love for Thornton seemed to grow and grow. Thornton, alone among men, could put things on Buck's back in the summer travelling. Nothing was too great for Buck to do when Thornton commanded.

"I shouldn't like to be the man that lays hands on Thornton while Buck's around," said Pete.

"I shouldn't either," Hans said.

Pete's fears were made real before the year had ended. They were at Circle City. "Black" Burton, an evil and unfriendly man, had been trying to quarrel with someone at the bar when Thornton stepped between the two men. Buck was lying in a corner, watching everything his master did. Burton suddenly struck out straight from the shoulder. Thornton was knocked back and saved himself from falling only by catching hold of the bar.

Those who were looking on heard a deep growl. They saw Buck's body rise up in the air as he jumped for Burton's throat. The man saved his life by holding out his arm, but he was thrown backwards to the floor with Buck on top of him. Buck stopped biting the arm and drove in again for the throat. This time the man did not completely succeed in stopping Buck's attack, and his throat was cut open. Then the crowd stopped Buck, and he was driven off. But while a doctor examined the man's throat, Buck walked up and down, growling angrily, attempting to rush in, and being forced back by several clubs.

The men called a "miners' meeting" there and then. They decided that the dog had had enough reason to attack the man, and Buck was set free. But after that everyone knew the kind of dog Buck was, and from that day his name spread through every camp in Alaska.

Later, towards the end of the summer, Buck showed his love for John Thornton in a different way. The three men were taking a long canoe down some dangerous rapids. Hans and Pete moved along the river bank, tying the rope of the canoe to one tree after another. Thornton remained in the canoe, steering it with a long oar and shouting orders to the bank. Buck ran along the bank, keeping level with the canoe. His eyes never left his master.

At an especially bad place where there were dangerous rocks in the river, Hans had untied the rope from one of the trees on the bank and was running with the end of the rope to tie it to the next tree. Thornton was trying to steer the canoe away from the bank, but the river took charge and turned it sideways. Hans pulled the rope to slow the canoe down, but he pulled it too suddenly. The canoe turned over, and Thornton was thrown into the water. The fast current carried him down the river towards the worst part of the rapids. There the water was thrown so wildly between the rocks that no swimmer could come out alive.

Buck jumped in at once. Three hundred metres down-stream he caught up with Thornton. When he felt Thorn-ton catch hold of his tail, Buck used all his splendid strength to swim straight towards the bank. But the return towards the shore was slow, and they were being carried quickly down the river. From below came the terrible sound of the water falling on the many rocks in the river. Thornton knew now that it was impossible to reach the shore. His body struck some rocks. He caught hold of the top of one rock with both hands. He was no longer holding Buck, and he shouted, "Go, Buck! Go!"

Buck was carried on by the racing river, struggling hard, but unable to stop himself. When he heard Thorn-ton's command a second time, he partly lifted himself out of the water, throwing his head high, as if for a last look. Then he turned towards the bank. He swam with all his great strength and was pulled out of the river by Pete and Hans just where the water began to flow over the worst of the rapids.

Pete and Hans knew that John Thornton could hold on to the wet rock for only a very few minutes and they ran as fast as they could up the bank to a place far above where he was hanging on to the rock. They tied a rope to Buck's neck and shoulders and put him into the stream. Buck began to swim without any fear at all. But he swam straight towards Thornton, not far enough out into the stream. He discovered the mistake too late, when he saw Thornton a few metres away to one side. The fast-flowing water carried Buck past without allowing him a chance to help.

Hans at once pulled the rope, as if Buck were a boat. The rope pulled him under the water, and he remained under the water until his body struck against the bank

Buck swims out to rescue Thornton

and he was lifted out. He was half drowned. Hans and Pete threw themselves on him, beating the breath into him and the water out of him. He struggled to his feet and fell down. The faint sound of Thornton's voice came to them. Though they could not hear his words clearly, they knew that he was very near death. The sound of his master's voice did something to Buck. He sprang to his feet and ran up the bank in front of the men to the place where they had put the rope round him before.

Again the rope was tied to Buck and again he started to swim, but this time straight out into the stream. Hans let out the rope. Buck swam straight out till he was on a line directly above Thornton. Then he turned and came downstream towards him. Thornton saw him coming. As Buck struck him with the whole force of the stream behind him, Thornton reached up and threw both his arms round Buck's neck. Hans put the rope round a tree, and Buck and Thornton were pulled under the water. Unable to breathe, and thrown violently against rocks, they moved in to the bank.

When Thornton became conscious, he was lying on his stomach. Hans and Pete had their hands on his back and were throwing their weight in a regular movement, trying to make him breathe. John Thornton's first anxiety was for Buck. There seemed to be no life in his body, and Nig was howling miserably over it. Skeet was moving her tongue over the wet face and closed eyes. Thornton was himself hurt badly, but he carefully examined Buck's body and found three broken bones in the powerful chest.

"That settles the matter," he said. "We camp right here." And they camped right there until Buck's bones were mended and he was able to travel.

Chapter 7
Buck hears the call

At last it was possible for John Thornton to go on a journey with his two friends into the east to search for a lost mine. The history of the mine was as old as the history of the country. Many men had looked for it; few had found it; and there were more than a few who had never returned from the search. This lost mine was covered in mystery. No one knew of the first man who found it: the stories about the mine stopped before they got back so far. From the beginning there had been an old hut. Dying men had talked about it, holding in their hands rocks of gold different from all the known types of gold in the Northland.

But no living man had taken gold from the mine, and the dead were dead. Therefore, John Thornton and Pete and Hans, with Buck and six other dogs, started into the east on an unknown path to succeed in doing something that other men and dogs as good as themselves had failed to do. They travelled seventy miles up the Yukon, swung east up Stewart River, and kept on until the river itself became a stream among the mountains.

John Thornton asked little of man or nature. He was unafraid of the wild. As he was in no hurry, he hunted his dinner in the course of a day's travel. If he failed to find any food, he kept on travelling, safe in the knowledge that sooner or later he would come to it. So, on this great journey into the east, dogs and men ate fresh meat.

To Buck the journey was full of endless delight: he loved this hunting and wandering through strange places.

For weeks at a time they travelled on, day after day, and for weeks they camped here and there, the dogs lying around idly and the men burning holes through ice and dirt in their search for gold. Sometimes they were hungry, sometimes they feasted like kings, according to their success in hunting. Summer arrived, and dogs and men carried loads on their backs, rowed across blue mountain lakes, and went up and down unknown rivers in narrow boats cut from the trees around them.

The months came and went, and they travelled this way and that way through unknown country, where no men had been. They crossed mountains and dropped into warm valleys below. After summer they entered a strange lake-country, sad and silent, where there was no sign of life – only the blowing of cold winds, the forming of ice, and the sad sound of waves on the shores.

They wandered on through another winter. Once, they came upon an old path cut through the forest, and the Lost Hut seemed very near. But the path began nowhere and ended nowhere, and it remained a mystery. Who had made it and why had he made it? Another time they found part of an old hut which had been used for hunting. Among some clothes John Thornton found an old gun. And that was all – nothing else to tell them about the man who long ago had built the hut and left the gun there.

Spring came on once more, and at the end of all their wandering they never found the Lost Hut. But they did find a broad valley where the gold showed like yellow butter across the bottom of the stream. They looked no farther. Each day's work brought them thousands of dollars in clean gold dust and rocks of gold. And they worked every day. The gold was put into strong bags, fifty pounds of gold in each bag. The bags were then put on top of one another like firewood outside their small hut. They worked like giants day after day.

There was nothing for the dogs to do, except to pull in the meat that Thornton killed. Buck spent long hours dreaming by the fire.

One night he suddenly sprang from sleep. The call of the wild came from the forest (or one note of it, for the call had many notes), clear as never before – a long-drawn howl. The howl was like, yet unlike, any noise made by a dog. And Buck knew it as a sound that he had heard before. He sprang through the sleeping camp and in silence ran through the woods. As he drew closer to the cry he went more slowly, till he came to an open place among the trees. Looking out, he saw a long, thin wolf, standing very upright with its nose pointed to the sky.

He had made no noise, yet the wolf stopped howling and tried to find him. Buck walked into the open, his body half bent and gathered together. Every movement showed a strange mixture of angry power and a desire for friendship. But the wolf fled at the sight of him. He followed, springing wildly, in a great desire to catch up with the wolf. Buck forced the wolf into a small valley where there were several fallen trees; these stopped the wolf from escaping and it turned round. It growled fiercely and showed its teeth.

Buck did not attack, but walked round the wolf in a circle and made friendly advances. The wolf did not trust Buck and was afraid. Buck weighed three times more than the wolf, while the wolf's head only just reached Buck's shoulder. Watching his chance, the wolf ran away and Buck pursued once more. Again the wolf was caught because he was in poor condition. He ran till Buck's head was at the side of his body. Then he turned round ready to fight, only to run away again at the first chance.

But in the end Buck succeeded; for the wolf, finding that no harm was intended, put his nose close to Buck's nose. Then they became friendly and played together. After some time the wolf started off at an easy run in a way which plainly showed that he was going somewhere. He made it clear to Buck that he wanted him to come. So they ran side by side through the dim light, straight up the dry river-bed towards the foot of the mountains.

Then they came down into a flat country where there were great unbroken spaces of forest and many streams. Through these great unbroken spaces they ran on, hour after hour. The sun rose higher and the day grew warmer. Buck was wildly glad. He knew he was at last answering the call, running by the side of his brother towards the place the call came from. Old memories were coming upon him fast, and he was moved by them as he had been moved by them in his dreams. But this time he was no longer dreaming: everything was real. He had done this thing before, somewhere in that other and dimly remembered world. And he was doing it again now, running free in the open, with the untouched earth under his feet and the wide sky over his head.

They stopped by a stream to drink, and Buck suddenly remembered John Thornton. He sat down. The wolf started on towards the place the call came from, then returned to him, put his nose to Buck's nose and tried to make Buck follow him. But Buck turned and started slowly back. For an hour the wild brother ran by his side, howling softly. Then he sat down, pointed his nose to the sky, and howled. It was a sad howl. As Buck continued on his way back, he heard it grow fainter and fainter until it was lost in the distance.

John Thornton was eating his dinner when Buck ran into camp and sprang upon him, knocking him over and biting his hand. While Buck was showing his great love for his master, John Thornton shook Buck and cursed him lovingly.

For two days and nights Buck never left camp and never let Thornton out of his sight. He followed him at his work, watched him while he ate, saw him to bed at night and saw him get up in the morning. But after two days the call in the forest began to sound more powerful than ever. Buck could not forget his wild brother and the run side by side through the wide forest spaces. Once again he began to wander in the woods, but the wild brother didn't come. Though he listened through long nights, the sad howl was never heard.

Buck began to sleep out at night, staying away from camp for days at a time. Once he went down into the land of the wide forest spaces and the many streams. He wandered there for a week, seeking without success for fresh signs of the wild brother. He killed his meat as he travelled and never seemed to tire. He fished in a broad stream and by this stream he killed a large black bear which had been blinded by insects and was running wildly through the forest, helpless and terrible. Even so, it was a hard fight. And two days later, when he returned to the dead bear and found a dozen small animals quarrelling over it, he frightened them so much that they ran away like the wind. But they left behind two who would quarrel no more.
His desire for blood became stronger than ever before.

He was a killer, a thing that killed to eat, living on the things that lived. And he killed alone, by his own strength, living in a land where only the strong could live. He was an animal who lived only on meat, and he was in full flower, at the height of his strength and power. Every part of his body was alive. To sights and sounds and events which demanded action, he answered with a speed that surprised everyone. He could spring twice as quickly as any other dog to defend himself from attack or to attack. He saw the movement, or heard a sound, and answered before other dogs had seen or heard anything. He saw and thought and answered in the same moment. Life ran through him and filled every part of his body. It seemed that there was not enough room for all the life that flowed through his body and that it would pour out over the world.

"There never was such a dog," said John Thornton one day, as they watched Buck marching out of camp.

They saw him marching out of camp, but they did not see the sudden and terrible change that happened as soon as he was in the forest. He no longer marched. At once he became a thing of the wild, moving softly like a cat. He was a passing shadow that appeared and disappeared among the shadows. He knew how to hide, to move on his stomach like a snake, and like a snake to spring and strike. No animals were too quick for him. He killed to eat, not from pleasure alone; but he liked to eat what he killed himself.

After summer had passed, the moose appeared, moving slowly down to meet the winter in the lower and warmer valleys. Buck had already killed a young moose which had wandered away from the others. Now he very much

61

wanted to hunt larger moose. He came upon a band of
twenty moose one day at the head of a small river. The
moose had crossed over from the land of streams and
forests. Chief among them was a great bull-moose. He
was an angry beast; he stood over six feet from the
ground; he was as terrible an animal as even Buck could
want to fight. The bull threw his head from side to side.
His small eyes burned with an evil light while he growled
with anger at the sight of Buck.

The feathered end of an arrow stuck out from the
bull's side – the reason for his fierce anger. Buck at once
knew what to do: he began to cut the bull out from the
rest of the band. It was not easy. He barked and danced
about in front of the bull, just out of reach of the powerful
head and the great feet which could have killed him with
a single blow. The bull was unable to turn his back on
Buck and go on, and became more and more angry. He
charged Buck; Buck drew back, making the bull think that
he could not escape. In this way he caused the bull to
follow him. But when the bull was separated from his
fellows, two or three of the younger bulls charged back
on Buck and helped the wounded bull to join the band
again.

Wild animals know how to wait. They do not hurry.
They wait for hour after hour till the right moment comes;
and then at last they strike. Buck knew how to wait. He
stayed at the side of the band of moose, slowing down
their march, making the young bulls angry, frightening
the cows with their young, and driving the wounded bull
mad with fierce but helpless anger. For half a day this
continued. All the moose became tired out. They could
not wait so long as Buck could wait.

As the day continued and the sun dropped to its bed in

the north-west, the young bulls grew less and less willing to go to the help of the old bull. The winter was driving them quickly to the valleys, and it seemed that they could never shake Buck off. Besides, it was not the life of the band of moose, or of the young bulls, that was in danger. It was the life of only one member. This did not hold the same interest for them as their own lives did, and they became less willing to help the old bull.

As night fell the old bull stood with his head held low, watching the rest of the band continue on their rapid journey. He could not follow, because in front of him jumped the terror which would not let him go. The great bull had lived a long, strong life, full of fight and struggle. At the end he faced death at the teeth of a creature whose head did not reach beyond his great knees.

From then on, night and day, Buck never left the old bull: he never gave him a moment's rest, never permitted him to eat the leaves of trees or to satisfy his burning thirst in the narrow streams they crossed. Sometimes the bull ran for a long time. At such times Buck did not try to stop him, but followed easily, satisfied with the way the game was played. He lay down when the moose stood still, and attacked him fiercely when he tried to eat or drink.

The great head dropped more and more, as the bull grew weaker and weaker. He began to stand for a long time, with nose to the ground and ears that dropped without any sign of strength. And Buck found more time to get water for himself and to rest. At such moments, with his red tongue hanging out and with eyes fixed on the big bull, Buck began to feel that a change was coming over the face of things. He could feel something new moving in the land. As the moose were coming into the land, other kinds of life were coming in. Forest and

Buck follows the old bull moose

stream and air seemed to beat with their presence. The news of it came to him, not by sight, or sound, or smell, but by some other, deeper feeling. He heard nothing, saw nothing, yet knew that the land was different in some way; and that through it strange things were moving. And he decided that he would see what was happening after he had killed the old bull.

At last, at the end of the fourth day, Buck pulled the great moose down. For a day and a night he remained by the dead bull that he had killed, eating and sleeping. Then, rested, refreshed and strong, he turned his face towards camp and John Thornton. He broke into the long, easy run and went on, hour after hour, returning straight home through strange country, completely certain of the direction.

As he continued, he felt more and more the new movement in the land. There was life in it, different from the life there had been through the summer. No longer did he know this fact in some deep, mysterious way. The birds and animals talked about it and the very wind whispered it. Several.times he stopped and drew in the fresh morning air in great breaths. It seemed to carry a message which made him run on with greater speed. He had the feeling that something terrible was happening, if it had not already happened. As he crossed the last stream and dropped down into the valley towards the camp, he ran with greater care.

Three miles away he came to a fresh path that filled him with fear. It led straight towards camp and John Thornton. Buck hurried on, quickly and quietly. Every sign told a story – all but the end of the story. He noticed the silence of the forest. The bird life had gone. The small creatures of the forest were hiding.

As Buck ran along like a silent shadow, his nose suddenly moved to the side as though a great force had pulled it. He followed the smell into a bush and found Nig. He was lying on his side, dead where he had pulled himself, an arrow sticking through his body.

A hundred yards farther on, Buck came upon one of the sledge-dogs that John Thornton had bought in Dawson. This dog was dying in great pain, and Buck passed around him without stopping. From the camp came the faint sound of many voices, rising and falling in a kind of song. Moving forwards on his stomach to the edge of the camp, Buck found Hans, lying on his face, with arrows sticking in his back. At the same moment Buck looked out at the place where the hut had been. He saw something that made his hair stand straight up on on his neck and shoulders. A great feeling of anger conquered. He didn't know that he growled, but he growled aloud – terrible and fierce. For the last time in his life he allowed his powerful feelings to conquer his reason: it was because of his great love for John Thornton that he lost control of himself.

The Indians were dancing around the remains of the small hut when they heard a terrible cry and saw Buck rushing upon them. Never before had they seen an animal like him. Buck's only desire was to destroy them as he threw himself on them. He sprang at the nearest man, who happened to be the chief of the Indians. In a second Buck's teeth had cut the man's throat wide open. He did not stop and, with the next jump, cut the throat of a second man. There was nothing the Indians could do. Buck sprang into the middle of them, never stopping in his destruction and moving so quickly that no arrows could hit him. In fact, his movements were so fast and the Indians were so closely gathered together, that they shot one another with the arrows. One young hunter, trying to throw a spear at Buck, drove it through the chest of another hunter with such force that the point broke through the skin of the back and stood out beyond it. Then the Indians turned and ran in terror to the woods, shouting out that the Evil Spirit had come.

And Buck really was like the Devil, pursuing them and pulling them down as they raced through the trees. It was a day the Indians would never forget. They ran far and wide over the country, and it was not until a week later that a few of them gathered together in a lower valley and counted their losses.

Tired of the pursuit, Buck returned to the camp. He found Pete where he had been killed in his bed in the first moment of surprise. On the earth there were the marks of Thornton's last struggle. Buck smelt every mark down to the edge of the stream. Skeet lay by the edge of the stream, head and front feet in the water – faithful to the last. The water of the stream was not clear and hid what it contained; and it contained John Thornton. Buck knew this, for he had followed the marks into the water from which no other marks led away.

Buck stayed by the stream all day or wandered about the camp. He knew what death meant, and he knew John Thornton was dead. It left a great empty space in him, rather like hunger, but it was a space that food could not fill. At times, when he stopped to look at the dead bodies of the Indians, he forgot the pain of it. At such times he felt a great pride in himself – a pride greater than any he had yet experienced. He had killed man, the noblest creature of all; and he had killed in the face of clubs. He smelt the bodies with curiosity. They had died so easily. It was harder to kill a wild dog than them. He could beat them easily if it were not for their arrows and spears and clubs. From then on he would not be afraid of them except when they carried in their hands their arrows, spears, and clubs.

Night came on. A full moon rose high over the trees into the sky, lighting the land. And as night came, Buck became alive to a moving of the new life in the forest. He stood up, listening and smelling. From far away there came a faint, sharp cry, followed by other sharp cries. As the moments passed the cries grew closer and louder. Again Buck knew them as things heard in that other world which he could not forget. He walked to the centre of the open space and listened. It was the call, the call with many notes: it was more commanding and more powerful than ever before. And as never before, he was ready to obey. John Thornton was dead. The last thing that tied him to the world of man was broken.

Hunting their living meat close behind the moose, the wolf pack had at last crossed over from the land of streams and forests and entered Buck's valley. Into the open space where the light of the moon fell, they poured in a stream of silver. And in the centre of the open space stood Buck. They were filled with fear; he stood so still and large. Not one of them moved for a moment. Then the bravest one sprang straight for him. At once Buck struck, breaking the wolf's neck. Then he stood, without movement as before. Three others tried it; and one after the other they drew back, blood pouring from cut throats or shoulders.

This was enough to throw the whole pack forwards, crowded together and so eager to pull Buck down that they were unable to think clearly. Buck's splendid quickness was a great help to him. Turning on his back legs and with his mouth quickly opening and closing, he was everywhere at once. But, to stop them from getting behind him, he was forced back, down to the stream. He moved along the bank to a place that the men had made while mining. Here he stood to face the wolves, protected on three sides, with nothing to do but face the front.

In this place Buck fought the wolves so well that at the end of half an hour they drew back. Their tongues were hanging out; their long white teeth showed cruelly white in the light of the moon. Some were lying down with heads raised and ears held forwards; others stood on their feet, watching him; and still others were drinking water from the stream. One wolf, long and thin and grey, advanced with great care, in a friendly manner. Buck recognised the wild brother that he had run with for a night and a day. He was howling softly, and, as Buck howled, they touched noses.

Then an old wolf, with many marks of battle on his body, came forward. Buck moved his lips in preparation for an angry growl, but smelt noses with him. Then the old wolf sat down, pointed his nose at the moon, and gave the long wolf howl. The others sat down and howled. And now the call came to Buck clearly. He, too, sat down and howled. When this was over, he came out from the bank and the pack crowded around him, smelling in a manner that was half friendly and half fierce. The leaders cried out and sprang away into the woods. The wolves followed, crying out together. And Buck ran with them, side by side with the wild brother, crying out as he ran.

Questions

Questions on each chapter

1 1 Why were men rushing to the north? (Because . . .)
   2 Who was Buck's first owner?
   3 Why did Buck allow Manuel to put a rope round his neck?
   4 What weapon did the man use for breaking in a dog?
   5 Who bought Buck after the breaking in?

2 1 What did "Mush!" mean?
   2 Where did the dogs sleep?
   3 How many dogs were in Perrault's team?
   4 What was Buck's daily food?
   5 Why did he learn to eat it quickly?

3 1 Which was Buck's great enemy among the dogs?
   2 Where did the strange dogs come from to attack the camp?
   3 What did François make for Buck?
   4 Which of the dogs went mad?
   5 What did François do to the mad dog?
   6 Where did Perrault's first journey end?
   7 How long was it before Perrault started back with the mail?
   8 Why did the whole team leave the camp one night?
   9 Which dog did better in the fight at first?
  10 Which dog won the fight?

4 1 What position in the team did Buck want – and get?
   2 Why were Perrault and François so proud in Skaguay?
   3 What was in the load when they started the journey back to Dawson?
   4 How long did the dogs have in Dawson?
   5 Which of the dogs became ill on the return journey?

5   1   How long did the journey from Dawson to Skaguay take?
      2   What did the drivers expect in Skaguay?
      3   What orders did they receive?
      4   Who bought Buck and his companions?
      5   Why couldn't the team move the sledge at first?
      6   Who was in a camp at the mouth of the White River?
      7   Why didn't the dogs get up when Hal ordered them to?
      8   What did Hal do to make them get up?
      9   Which dog refused to get up?
   10   What happened to the men and dogs of Hal's team?

6   1   What was John Thornton waiting for?
      2   What feeling was there between Buck and John Thornton?
      3   How did Thornton and his friends continue the journey to Dawson?
      4   Who hit Thornton in a bar?
      5   What happened to the man?
      6   Why wasn't Buck killed?
      7   Why did John Thornton fall into the river?
      8   What mistake did Buck make when he swam with the rope the first time?
      9   What did (a) Nig and (b) Skeet do when Buck was unconscious?
   10   What harm had the rocks done to Buck?

7   1   What did John Thornton and his friends set out to look for?
      2   How did they get food for men and dogs?
      3   What did they find in the end?
      4   Why did Buck run out of the camp one night?
      5   What was making the sound?
      6   What made Buck go back?
      7   What big animal did he want to hunt?
      8   How long did it take Buck to end his hunt?
      9   What signs made Buck hurry back to camp?
   10   What had happened to Hans?
   11   What happened to the Indians' chief?
   12   Why couldn't the Indians shoot Buck?
   13   What did they think Buck was?
   14   Where was John Thornton's body?
   15   Which of the wolves was friendly in the end?

Questions on the whole story

These are harder questions. Read the Introduction, and think hard about the questions before you answer them. Some of them ask for your opinion, and there is no fixed answer.

1   Which of Buck's human masters do you like best? Can you give a reason or reasons for your answer?

2   Which of the human masters do you like least? Again, can you give reasons?

3   Put the names of the dogs in the list into the first of four columns. In the second column, try to say whether you "Like" or "Dislike" the dog. In the third column, say why. In the fourth column, say what happened to the dog in the end. We have answered for Skeet as an example.
The dogs: Dave, Spitz, Sol-leks, Pike, Dolly.

1	2	3	4
Skeet	Like	John Thornton's dog, very friendly to Buck	Killed by Indians

4   Find the words in the book, keep the book open, and answer the questions that follow the words.
   a   "I get only fifty for it, and I wouldn't do it again for a thousand."
       1   Who is speaking?
       2   Where is he?
       3   What does he mean by "it"?
       4   What does he mean by "fifty"?
       5   Why wouldn't he like to do it again?
   b   "Three hundred, and he's a gift at that price. And it's government money that you're spending."
       1   Who is the speaker? (We don't know his name. Describe him.)
       2   Who is he speaking to?
       3   Where are they?
       4   What is the meaning of "he's a gift at that price"?
       5   Why is the money "government money"? (What is it being spent for?)

c   "Run on, poor feet. This is the last. Then we'll get a long rest."

   1 Who shouts these words?
   2 Where is he?
   3 Where has he come from?
   4 Who or what is he shouting to?
   5 Why don't they get a "long rest"?

d   "If you strike that dog again, I'll kill you."

   1 Who is the speaker?
   2 Who is he speaking to?
   3 Where are they?
   4 Which "dog" is meant?
   5 Why has the dog been struck?

New words

bark
(make) the sharp, loud
noise of an excited dog

bull-moose
a male **moose** (see below)

canoe
a boat of the kind used by
North American Indians

classic
a work of art (writing, etc)
that will always be
considered good

club
a heavy wooden stick, thick
at one end, used as a
weapon

growl
(make) a deep rough sound
in the throat to show anger
or give warning

harness
leather bands that fasten an
animal to the thing it is
pulling

moose
a kind of very large deer
with big flat horns, found in
the northern parts of North
America (and called an **elk**
in some northern countries
of Europe)

pack
a hunting group (of wolves
or wild dogs)

rapids
a place where a river runs
fast over and between rocks

sledge
a vehicle with runners
instead of wheels, used for
taking heavy loads across
snow

sympathy
understanding and sharing
other people's feelings